Flash Fiction

Flash Fiction

Craige Reeves

VANTAGE PRESS
New York

This is a work of fiction. Any similarity between the names and characters in this book and any real persons, living or dead, is purely coincidental.

Cover design by Polly McQuillen

FIRST EDITION

Copyright © 2005 by Craige Reeves

Published by Vantage Press, Inc.
419 Park Ave. South, New York, NY 10016

Manufactured in the United States of America
ISBN: 0-533-15053-1

Library of Congress Catalog Card No.: 2004097251

0 9 8 7 6 5 4 3 2

Flash Fiction

The Jungle #1

I roam the jungle. I've got a knife. I've got a spear. But, I'm lost. One path is the same as three hundred paths before it. Or, three hundred paths to come. I'm sick of it. Rivers look alike. Mountains seem the same. So, once, for awhile—I think it was for three years, and this was like, five years ago, I put notches in trees. The only problem is, I can't find any notches. Did they grow back over? And then one day—I saw one! And I said, "Who put that there?" I said, "Someone's here." Then I started laughing because I thought: "What's a notch for, anyway?"

The Jungle #2

Yeah, I roam the jungle. I've got a knife and a spear and I'm very lost. But I'm not scared. Yet. By my reckoning, I've been out in the jungle maybe two generations. Forty years. Forty long beautiful, wonderful years—in city measurements—but we're talkin' jungle. No cement. No car. No store. If I was scared, I'd be scared no one would find me—but, I'm not about to relinquish my courage, quite this soon. . . .

The Jungle #3

I'm pulling out all the stops. My name is George Lucas and I'm scratching words on bark. I'm lost and hope someone remembers me—or helps me find the way out of the jungle. I'm quite old. Perhaps a bit 'daft.' Perhaps a great deal! I don't think I was always lost in this @#& jungle. Every day, every night—hang on to spear; knife—knife; spear—every day; every night. I'm beginning to feel rather 'peaked' . . . I'm scared I'm nuts.

I heard something say, "If you put ten monkeys in a room with a computer, they'll eventually be able to write the collected works of Shakespeare on the head of a pin!"

What's a computer?

The Jungle #4

I guess what you would call me is an 'old fogey.' I trek through the jungle, as my bones permit. I say mantras, knife–spear; spear–knife. I took to making traps and snares. It's not an uncomfortable life; if you don't miss coffee and the news—or, if you like, tea and crumpets. . . . I saw a gouge out of a tree the other day. It stirred an old memory. . . .

The Ditch #1

'The Ditch' is growing longer and deeper. Deeper and longer. I will not call 'The Ditch' a canal. I will not call 'The Ditch' a gully. I will not call 'The Ditch' anything but 'The Ditch'!

When it rains, the sides of 'The Ditch' slide to the bottom and are moved right along; lickety-split in the flow of water from the rain. In the Spring, the cold melting snow runs through 'The Ditch,' eroding it, more and more.

I like to see the wind and rain carry some of 'The Ditch' away. In a generation, 'The Ditch' could be a culvert, or arroyo. The good thing about 'my' 'Ditch'—they're all over the place. The bad thing about this particular ditch is that one Spring my wife was collecting Daffodils and a sudden storm blew up and carried her away in this ditch!

The Ditch #2

As Barbara was sucked under the swollen 'Ditch,' she tried to yell. It was a drowning gurgle. I had been watching her pick Daffodils for us. She'd wandered too close to the bank. I'd tried to warn her; but, the roar of the muddy water drowned out my voice. The bank of 'The Ditch' slid into the water and Barbara with it! 'B-B-Bob!' A moan. A gurgling moan! I tried to grab her hand. I nearly jumped in the rapidly flowing water. The water swept her from my sight in moments. She was never found. My Barbara.

So I kick dirt in 'The Ditch'! I shovel dirt in 'The Ditch'! I pitch handful after handful of dirt in that son of a witch of a 'Ditch' . . . I'll bury it; bury it. . . .

The Tree

I was driving through rural Vermont; and I was suddenly no longer driving through rural Vermont.

I had just reached the top of long climb of a road and suddenly I was overlooking a picturesque valley. I'm a photographer in 'real-time,' and I know picturesque. There is a field at the bottom of Gilbert Hill in rural Vermont. And it is breathtaking. Daffodils fill the field. There are Crocuses. And Irises. But above and beyond all this, there was a tremendously huge 'Weeping Willow' tree, hung with long golden tendrils of vine.

This magnificent tree is just inside a row of crack-troop 'Soldier' trees. And as I studied this 'Glory-Scene', a chill ran through me. This was no accident of nature; the 'Weeping-Willow' tree wasn't being protected; it was being guarded. . . .

I Second That Thought

Ya' heard of Nanosecond? Well, what I want you to focus your attention on is Micro-second. Like if something happened in a Micro-second—ziiip. See ya. Adios. Let us presume lightning strikes in a Micro-second. One thing is true; it strikes 'in a flash.' Bummer.

But what of heating coffee in a *Micro*-wave oven? Thirty seconds—over easy? And buster, that coffee is scorching. Micro-second can be a great thing. But, like Micro-wave; Nano-second; Ultra-waves and Ultra-sound, with the 'ol Laser comin' along, we can just dot all the 'eyes' and cross all the 'tees' in this day and age on our Handy-Andy; Laser Matrix Dot Printer!

But I'm a defeatist. I'm thinking Laser range weaponry . . . uh-oh; I've got a cavity—I hope they don't fill it with some Microchip they find laying around.

Bookworm

Did ya' ever hear of a 'Silver-Fish'? They're as fast as greased lightning and almost invisible. But, wherever there's a stack of old newspapers or books, especially since the dark ages? There'll be Silver-Fish.

They seem like Centipedes, but silver. Duhh. They never bit me. Not even a little. Like, they're more scared of you than . . . they're shy. But I don't want to make a pet out of one of them regardless. So, anyway, all this to say I'm a Bibliophile. I love books. Sue me. I'd be a bookworm, though—not a Silver-Fish.

The Pit #1

I circled the pit, nearly blind. I had been blindfolded, but I had loosened it by rubbing it against the wall. The pit is cylindrical, hence—pit. I could not loosen the blindfold because Nemo had cut my arms off. You think I'm kidding? I'm writing this with my mouth. He put pen and paper here to make me squirm. Poor Nemo; John won't squirm.

He threw down duct tape. Told me to choke myself with it. Get it over with quick. He had knocked me out with ether and he then injected me with Novocain; 100c.c.— every four hours. We'll have no O.D. in my pit.

The big hearted S.O.B. The worst of my suffering, aside from pain, was taping these notes to the rats. Ever hold down a sewer rat with your chin while you diligently tape on the note with your mouth? I'll never proffer my left hand to be shook as a joke again.

The Pit #2

It's John again. Nemo has more tricks in his skull than sense. He put cages in the pit. I was what? Supposed to stop him? Didn't ya hear? He's got a cross–cut saw and no sense of humor.

He keeps me in one or another of the four cages. Count 'em (1–2–3–4) not three cages; not five cages; but four cages; so I can have a 'room–with–a–view.' This angle as opposed to that angle.

Nemo has a loose screw. Yeah, he's a beaut. So anyway Nemo sez to me one day, "Maybe I'll lay the cages down." And I'm thinking, don't even go there; and I SAY, "Why not take the cages out and ya can can watch me walk around in circles?"

Nemo liked the idea . . . so far, so good.

The Pit #3

It's probably because of the rats but I have no appetite. I avoid water; and good 'ol Nemo gives me a shot of something every other day.

It's got to be for one of two things—Tetracycline—for disease. I'm thinking rabies. Or Quinine—for dysentery. 100 c.c.s. We'll have no O.D. in my pit.

Exotic rats. But now, I got a killer rash. I rub the wall front and back. I rub the wall back and front. But, it's a funny thing . . . what I thought was moss—it's kinda growin' on me like some kinda fungus and it itches.

Lord it itches. . . .

The Pit #4

It's me, John, and I'm back in control. Nemo put a broad in here with me. She's hysterical and I can't slap her to end the hysterics; but, she itches the rash.

I had to tell her to touch me. No sickness here. We're talkin' survival.

Anyway her sin against Nemo must not have ben quite as bad as mine because—she's got all her working parts.

I called her a broad when I started this note because Nemo cut the rations. So what we've stooped to . . . me and girl; a bite here . . . and a bite there.

Did I say you can block pain??? Girl will grow used to it. . . .

Pestilence

Ja' ever get a bug up your butt about something that just wouldn't seem to let up no matter how much ya worried at it???

Well, I kinda got a bit of a Godzilla suppository kickin' my butt a good one. It's Peg. Ya'd think she was the only one-legged ass kicker in town. Geeez. Exxxcuse me.

I tol' her a long time ago I was gonna start callin' her Peg—but affectionately like. Was it my fault, all of a sudden like, that she didn't see the train coming that fateful shroud-encountered night when her first stew-bum ole man was passed out in the back seat and lost his head over her???

Yeah, come to think of it, they won't let me drive trains no more!!!

The Burr

Being saddled with a younger brother when the older kids are running around playing football or baseball outside is really no big deal—if you tie him to a tree!

I hate my younger brother; but I would never hurt him or let anyone else ever hurt him either. I'll never let him know it though.

Besides, half the time—he's nowhere around.

"Johnny, have you seen Paul?"

"No, Mom."

It was Summer. School vacation. The best time for rammin' around; but you don't want your kid brother stuck to you.

One day Paul comes running up. "Johnny, get the guys. You gotta see this."

It was in Mr. Samson's garage. At first I thought it was a red and brown rug. Then I saw the red was running independently across the garage floor. A dead deer.

"Did Mister Samson kill it, Johnny?"

"I don't know, squirt."

This was getting better and better. The stench was awful and there were a thousand flies. The side door to the garage/house suddenly flew open and a pasty complexioned Mrs. Samson came running through the open door yelling, "Get away from my 'Road-Kill'!!!"

The Dance

It was supposed to be an enactment of the Dance of the Dead. Hardly THAT. Drug abused hippy stand-ins??? They dragged their feet. The dead 'drifted.' They bumped into one another. Real dead 'interlaced.' It was a sham. Hocus-Pocus.

Harold could do what these fools shamed themselves doing and at least act convincing!!!!

The last of the applause died down and Harold made his move. Weighing only ninety-six pounds he curled his frame in a ball and grabbed his shins. He would stay in the row of seats in which he was the only occupant; in his seat hardly bulging outward—until the theater emptied.

An hour later when he had re-rigged the proper lighting—the proper sound—the proper sets, he danced. Harold did. He put his heart and soul into it—to a theatre empty of people.

Then—clapping! "Bravo, Mister Haroldson, Bravo."

"Wh—Who's there?"

"You have nothing to fear from me, Mr. Haroldson. You must face and fear the inner critic."

All Harold could see from whence the voice sprang, (he allowed himself a slight humorless chuckle), was a wisp of smoke!!! Steeling himself, Harold spoke again. "I asked you who you are!!!"

"I am death, Mister Haroldson," the wisp spoke.

"What do you want???" Harold could feel himself getting ugly. Ninety-six pounds or not, he was ounce for ounce a scrapper.

The vapor spoke for the last time. "To tell you, Mr. Haroldson, that you're riddled with carcinoma!!!"

Pop Dispenser

I don't feel good and I haven't felt good 'lo these many moons. It's that soda jerk is who it is.

Shake Shake. Fizz Fizz. Oh, what a relief it is!!! Well, also unwell put; 'I'm all shook up.' The jerk fillin' me up with shook to shucks soda—is makin' these cans open up in me—a lower than life Pop machine nobody gives a second thought about. BUT—the spillage of carbonated acid has what you may describe as having crossed my 'Wires'!!!

I've got myself pretty well put together as of late—I don't feel good . . . but, I'm gonna 'FIX' mister whistling soda jerk hisself!!! It's sorta sad, but wait; he's commin'. Kabboom.

The Thing in the Wall

The noise Eric thought he heard in the wall the first time, he thought was his imagination. By the tenth or eleventh time, Eric was pretty certain there was a little something behind the peeling plaster in the kitchen.

This apartment he lived in used to be nice. Now, Eric had claimed squatter's rights six or seven months ago. The drugs did that. They clouded up his thoughts. He didn't remember when he last ate—he was always hungry and it was bitter in the dark boarded-up old house.

He had a loose board in what used to be a window. He could come and go at will. Sometimes the panhandling on Ober Street produced enough change for a pint of gin. All in all, things weren't real bad. He looked around the naked kitchen and spotted something he could use to dig the wall open with. A metal table leg.

After he steeled his courage with a healthy slug of gin, from his last bottle, Eric swung the bar at the wall like it was a bat and he had a chance at the winning run. There suddenly arose in the kitchen such a vile, fetid stench, Eric felt his gorge rise. "Whaaaat????" He had finally found his long-lost mother.

Xavier

I am Xavier ant and nobody knows it. I saw a fly in a spider web shouting himself to death for help. I saw armies of ants like me attack armies of ants like them—and die.

I am a smart ant. People, ants, spiders—nobody and nothing likes a smart ant. I keep to myself. I've seen ant hives and ant colonies torn apart and destroyed by a rotten boy's sneaker. A reckless lawnmower.

I've got leaves, twigs, a source of water, and no one understands that. I have this stuff in my part of the hive. To have it makes me feel important. I did not ask to be able to think, but how so very liberating!!! How free!!!

I take things I want. I take chances. I take ants' lives. I take ants. And I take ants' things. Then I made a mistake. A big mistake. I stepped in poison, and, since I didn't want to die alone, I made a beeline for the hive; the trail of which the spiders came home on.

The Locket

Lois looked over at Stanley again. She had looked over at him ten times in ten minutes. There was no doubt about it; they were going to be late—and on the day Stanley had gotten his hard won promotion. "Stanley, we're going to be late."

He was alternately sipping scotch from a big tumbler full, puffing a fat cigar, and trying to tie a tie. "It's okay, Lois, nobody's ever on time." Stanley's belly stuck out in front of him like a 'stuffed shirt'; in this case—literally.

At least he'd brushed his teeth, Lois had thought on the way over to the Thomases, Stanley's boss. They wouldn't have to smell the booze or cigar. And she thought with a wry grin, he spared me that unpleasantness, also.

Maybe Lois hadn't been invited to a lot of office parties, she thought, and she didn't think Mary Thomas got invited to a lot of them either; at least not as a guest but possibly as a hostess. Lois had a sense of the proper things to do in life. Like bringing a gift when calling on someone. She'd brought her mother's locket to Mrs. Thomas. It was an obsidian profile Cameo locket.

Mrs. Thomas said, "Is it plastic?" At which point Lois threw her in the pool.

The Hands

The Hands were around my throat again; which, in and of itself, would not be horrible. But, this guy's knee was pushing down on my solar-plexus. The hair on his knuckles signified he is a man. My hands are tight tight around his wrists—trying to pull them off my throat. I'm sweating profusely.

My name is John Lucas and this R.E.M. nightmare happens with the guy's face a blur; yet it's less than a foot from my straining, bulging eyes.

I explained this to my psychiatrist one day and he said, "Are you sure it was your solar–plexus he was pushing on and not your sternum???" Jesus.

I was arrested the next day and sentenced to die for first-degree murder because I'd bought a gun, shot the intruder in my R.E.M. nightmare in the face, which passed through the ceiling of my bedroom and into my seventy-two-year-old neighbor's stomach upstairs. He died.

The Foot

My brother's foot was kicking me awake again. Subconsciously in R.E.M. Nightmare. I smelled it coming in to kick me.

My name is Roger Roberts. My brother John lost his foot in Korea. Gangrene. They say the Doughboys in World War I had trench mouth; and, for some un-Godly reason, I equate 'Trench-Mouth' with 'Hoof-n'-Mouth' disease; and, my brother John kicking the shit out of me.

"Roger, get up, it's time for breakfast." John was tousling my hair in brotherly love, and untypical affection. Very untypical.

"When you're done with chow, you're on clean-up detail!!!"

The Dust Mote

I'm a dust mote. There is no other explanation for one moment looking up from a shaft of sun/moon light, to looking down at a base heater, at the junction of a floor and a wall, to feeling yourself expunged from someone's (or something's) (God, not a dog's) nose, at heart attack speed all wet behind the sneeze—that you're Not a mote.

I'm in someone's brain. I was in their eye and they rubbed and soaped and watered me right into their nerve center. What's so good about THIS is, we're gaining dead weight mass. Sorta like mud. I'm thinking of making conduits; and rivulets; and canals, using this brain. I think I'll make myself laugh—

"Beware the Mote."

The Party

"Harvey, I'm scared." And Susan WAS scared. She had a right to be. "There's going to be drugs at Harry's." Harvey's brother's house. They were only teenagers, but the guys in the group were thrill seekers.

"Cool it babe, you'll be fine." Harvey smirked inwardly thinking how he had just told Susan she was not much more than a commodity.

The house had been a boarded-up, derelict farmhouse out in the country; before Harry had claimed unofficial ownership. There was lighting provided by propane lanterns; candles and flashlights. Several huge metal tubs filled with ice contained all the beer and liquor twenty kids could get drunk on, and the air was acrid with sweet hemp smoke. Pills were taken.

At some point, Susan was stripped and tied down on a table. She said, "Harvey, I'm scared." She started to smoke. Visible currents of electricity began to bold from her and then she caught on fire; blew up; and disappeared.

The official report was: Spontaneous Combustion!!!

The Writer

I'm a pen. I know. I know. Horse shup. And yet you hold the proof before your face!!! What's with you humans??? Were you all born stupid??? Starting with the date in the upper right for a couple centuries, what? I wasn't supposed to what? Learn to measure time??? Oh no, I'm running out of ink—I'm running out of time. . . .

The Web

I'm ant. You can call me Zar.

It is true an ant is one hundred times stronger than the relationship of size/strength ratio. I came on a web one day. A spider web. Is there another kind? The web was small small. That's okay, because I'm a tiny ant.

Something came over me. I thought I'd smash it-pull it apart. Mistake!!!

Beginning with a single strand, I managed to unhook that strand it was anchored to on a bush stem. I suddenly got the idea to stretch open the end of 'said strand,' and climb within. It immediately closed over me.

Nature Call

Don't help us! We're the sick insects of the group. The ones stepped on and still alive you try to 'help.' Do us a favor—don't do us any favors. As you humans say, When one of us are *'down'* a distress signal goes out and we are similarly picked up and dispatched. We are beheaded in the mandibles of the rescuer—if we're lucky. But you!! You! With your human stench; your human residue. Your odor!!! When it comes near us it is here to stay. The gum you had last week is as fresh a stink on us as if you had it a moment before. The scout doesn't just behead us as much as pull off our various limbs.

Bad Man

"Ma, what's a bad man?"

"Why, Billy? Where did you hear about a 'Bad-Man'?"

Martha was doing the lunch dishes and she glanced back, frowning at her precocious six-year-old. "Well, Daddy said you got to 'stick 'em up for yourself,' " he misquoted his father.

Barbara Collins smiled inwardly. 'Macho' William R. Collins would raise his son as brave as himself—or there was the dickens to pay. He kept a roof over their heads. He had an insurance policy, and a rather large annuity plan, so all in all, things weren't so bad.

She sat in a chair behind her son, who lay on the floor with his head propped on his hands, elbows connected to the floor, arms somewhat like the arms of 'dubba-voos' —and sighed.

If only Billy knew. *Could* know. His 'ol man would get out of the 'CrowBar' hotel soon enough.

The Room

The Victorian mansion sat alone on ten acres of land covered on three sides by a dense woods. In the Winter the treetops glistened with snowfall. In the Summer a lush canopy of greenery sat atop the woods.

The mansion boasted thirty-two rooms. Twelve bedrooms. Ten bathrooms. There is a big dining room, two living rooms, four game rooms. There is a huge kitchen, and there is Thelma. Thelma is as an integral part of Mongus Mansion on rural route 378 in Manchester County, Pennsylvania, as everything else about this colossus. In the house library (as Mr. Lloyd Mungus, the first owner liked to call it), Thelma quickly dusted. There was a party tonight!

Mister Mungus and all his associates would be there! Thelma could smell the turkey roasting in the oven as tonight's main course. Thelma was so excited. Mr. Mungus had 'High Color' at these affairs.

Thelma Mungus had had a nervous breakdown. Dr. Thomas said she'd recover as she overcame the hallucinations associated with her husband having passed away.

Carelessness

Carelessness costs. Carelessness costs but I need money. My old lady needs an operation. Good time to need an operation. No consideration is what I'd call it. Pretty damn inconsiderate and inopportune is something else I'd call needing the ole blue paper suits including hats routine.

Okay, I'm a junkie and I can't jones down off the horse. Sue me. But would I go in the hospital about it? Hell no—I'd take all the drugs—and you don't want to know how many other hard cases told me that same story as I'm telling me and you. You just don't want to know.

Somethin' else too. Joan don't need need to be in the hospital. She's like one 'o them hypoconoures. She donates body parts. One day I can come home pretty much lit up an' wanna do a little gittin' it on—and she's missin' a friggin' kidney!!! A friggin' kidney. And I gotta go visiting hours! One time she was missing an eyeball! An eyeball!!! An' I gotta' be Mister Nice Guy and bring her flowers!

Well, piss on your flowers, Jones or Joan or joune . . . I need a fix. . . .

Slow Endings

I've been assistant Librarian for three years. Three long beautiful years that seem like one long love affair. I stock shelves with new books. Vacuum. Dust. In the Winter I shovel. In the Summer I mow. Harper Library on Miramar Lane is rustic, rural Hanharper, Maine boasts a one-hundred-foot sidewalk, (I shovel), and a twenty-acre lawn, (I mow).

As I said, I love my job. Nothing about one part of my job(s) stands out more than any other part(s) of my job, it's that some of what I do—I relish. It's Salley Renfield on a warm spring morning before her hair is up in a utilitarian bun which "is proper for a young Head Librarian," according to town council members. That I relish.

I love Saturdays. Saturdays at the library is kids' day. There's a huge Weeping Willow tree in the center of the lawn. Me and the kids sit under it and I tell them stories. I tell their parents to pack them a PB&J sandwich for a snack. I bring some for the kids that don't have one.

This is my favorite story for the boys and girls that come around.

Books are made out of paper. I don't know anybody who doesn't like paper. Sometimes people put money in books. I've heard of people who tape ten and twenty dollar bills to both sides of a page in a book—throughout the entire book!!! *Wealthy* people.

You'd be surprised what I get from these dopey kids.

Homework

You would think that after maybe the seventh or eighth test Mr. Bower gave me, he'd know I didn't *know* sex education! My parents are Prespitarian, and real prudish about subjects like that. "When you need to know, Mary, we'll tell you." It none the less hurt to be kept in the dark about 'the wonder of it all.' Especially with Billy Burke, what with his t-shirt sleeves rolled up to display bulging biceps and triceps and imagining them wrapped tightly around my straining, yearning, aching body.

Mary felt herself flush beet red as Mr. Bowers passed out the eighth or ninth failing grade to her. "Mister Bowers, excuse me." Mary would have to be calm but firm.

"Yes, Mary, what is it?" Mr. Bowers was acting coy, Mary saw, as though being imposed upon. For the benefit of the rest of the class?

"Don't you like me, Mr. Bowers?" Mary asked regrettably.

"See me after class, Mary," he said abruptly.

"I like you very much, Mary," Mr. Bowers stated after classes were through for the day. Mary was seated primly in front of his desk. "Yes, indeed, Mary. But you're the type of person someone of my generation would label 'a good girl.' And that's rather unfortunate—for you."

"What do you mean?" Mary asked quietly.

"Because, Mary, you're shy, naive, and it's got quite an effect on the boys in school, and Mary, we just can't have that. Not in MY school."

Blockhead

I felt invigorated. I had worked my eight-hour shift at 'Poke 'n Choke,' my buddy Jeff's nickname for 'Mcee-Dees.'

"Poke the eyes out of those eggs when you make a breakfast sandwich in MY restaurant, mister." Which didn't come close to mattering to begin with, as Jeff and I worked four to closing.

"Want to run over to Al's and have a couple of Buds with me?" Jeff asked with a sly grin. "There's a lot of loose women, Carmen." I smiled, flipped him the bird, and said, "Later."

I had worked very hard and I was quite tired, (it's not easy to work in public) but, it was a good tired. It was snowing out. It was December 3rd. And I felt liberated. I was moving fast. That's when I went down! Ice! White Ice! Ka-Boom. I landed on my back—so I got off lucky. I pride myself on wide firm shoulders—but man that hurt. I got the wind knocked out of me.

Once my nerves settled a little, I headed home again. A good deal more cautiously. That's when I almost got jumped. Actually, it got me motivated to truck on out and get home in time for the late show. After I was on my way again voices cut me up about having, 'Nose dived.' About being a bumbler. Which is when a police cruiser came slowly down the street and the heckling, jeering, and name calling came to an immediate end.

Man 'O' Man

The last time I saw O'Malley we were in 'Big Water,' as O'Malley himself was fond of calling anything out at sea further than 100 Nautical miles. Yeah, it was a 'Ray' that did it in for Ray O'Malley. I don't know what that lob was doing that far out at Sea and I don't want to know. I'm just glad to be on dry land.

R–A–J–I–F–O–R–M–S, the order of Manta Ray of the Greek Radjidae family.

We'd heard a thud under the boat a week or two before the storm of the year that Summer and I swear that when Ray was thrashing around in the water with that Man 'O' War or whatever the hell it was, there was a scarlet gash three feet wide in its thick hide on its back.

Well, whatever that brute was, it was might–y–y–y mad. It come at O'Malley tail-end first. It impaled him. It shook him loose. Then it impaled him again. I still hear Ray screaming in my nightmares.

And now I think you know a Manta Ray as opposed to a Man 'O' War may be as different as male and female?

Work

I kept watching Jimmy's mouth working up an' down on that gum thinking, 'How the hell could I have been scared of this geek?'

"That it?" Jimmy asked around his mouthful of gum, "Ya just gotta change a number of sumthin'?" Jimmy was asking me about writing. I'd told him that you could start off a story—"Let's say, d–o–g, Jimmy." And then have a sequence or, if you prefer, sexual. Dog 1. Dog 11. Or sumptin'.

We weren't working with Einstein with Jimmy, but it was going to be a ball milking a bit of loot out of him. And the best part? He won't even know it. No. No Shakespeare, Jimmy. In the guise of tutorialship, I sent him packing with a stern admonishment to show me current works in progress.

The way I had this planned out, Jimmy would bring me the next great "War and Peace," and on a simplistic pretext dismiss his chance at the brass ring, offer to trash it for him, change the title, author—that would be me mind you—and voilá.

Jimmy called me over to his house and said he had something for me. The first time he hit me with the bat he said, "This is dog one, this is dog eleven. . . ."

"Ice Capades"

We decided after that all night poke game us guys would just love to be out on the ice catching (hack) pan fish, (Brrr), roughing it, (it's a man thing, hon, you wouldn't understand) pneumonuing it—more like, and just in general making dummies out of ourselves.

Well, we bored a hole in the ice just like those textbook pictures showed us happy as you please—and then, silly as you please, a couple 'o us cussers started to take a dunken. Now I don't really care one way or the other about it so much as I was a wee bit under the weather to begin with, so, I helped Jimmy out and I started thinking as they made a human chain—hands to feet—to pull ME out, what would happen if they all started licking and kissing the ice all of a sudden. Their tongues and lips would freeze to the ice in a split second is what would happen!

And then I thought 'Change the subject Bubba, 'cause there's a weird chemistry about the Law of Nature or something that you best not set in motion in your mind less somebody doesn't fish you outta this pond 'til Spring.'

The Agenda

I quit smoking and drinking a good three years ago. I'll never walk on water, but, maybe just maybe, I'll live until I'm over one hundred years old—if I watch my diet—my exercise. Now, I quit smoking cold turkey—I thought I'd go bonkers. Booze was different. It took me thirty years to get sober for four years. Dry is what I tell everybody. I may not be sober for twenty years—if ever.

I once thought that if you totally recovered you could write a self-help book or be an actual therapist in a rehab, or counselor. Actually you can do anything you make up your mind to do—within reason. So, I gave up drinking every day—gradually—and a three-pack-a-day grunge and I started to ride a bike I got for my fifty-seventh birthday.

Now I ain't gonna tell you I got the lungs of a ten-year-old, or even a forty-year-old; but I cover ground, haul ass, as my ma would say. And I have some endurance. I can comfortably ride five miles, fish at the lake I end up at, and make it home to clean the fish, and watch the Yankee game.

But, I got into the junk. Ten times? Fifteen??? This sucks even talking about it. When *I* went to rehab, they told me you could get holes in your lungs. Well, I figured, maybe because I'd had such limited contact with that shit, I'd luck out. Then the therapists and counselors started talking about anniversaries, and cycles, relapse . . .

The Same Crowd

I wouldn't say I'm what you'd call, a' Lot Lizard,' but a great many things appeal to me when the sun goes down. Booze. Women—and yeah, yeah the later it gets the better they look; blah, blah, blah. Booze—did I say booze?? A cigar at night is a luxury often overlooked even by a 'Coinsurer.'

I hold to the old school in that—a place for all—all in its place. I retract my earlier statement that I'm no 'Lot Lizard.' I'm far, far worse. I'm a predator. I'm a stalker. I'm as sick as they get. I'll be caught. And I'll practice my perversions in the joint.

My thinking was screwed up even when I was a kid. Recurring nightmare, you understand. In this recurring nightmare my ma and dad are going at it 360 degrees. Well anyway, some things get lost in the translation, but I'm placed under my mother's back as part of the excitement. Well, my ma doesn't want me to suffocate and therefore keeps her hips raised.

So I burn the shit out of "men" with those big fat cigars I love at night during full moons. And I whip "men" naked of skin with coat hangers. So, yeah, I'm a Lot Lizard.

The Bell Jar Effect

The Bell Jar Effect was a mystery to Professor Dublin from the moment we used it on Project 10. We were trying to isolate a cold virus in a vat of dry ice. Now of course cold viruses and viruses of all sorts had been isolated and neutralized many many times. The trick it seemed with Project 10 was, dry ice is unstable. We scientists at Outreach 8, Antarctica, had limited resources to define a neutralization and/or Bell Jar Effect on a virus in extreme conditions; and it was imperative that we do so, fast—if not sooner.

One of the crew had come down with a bad case of pneumonia and we had then injected him with 4c.c.s of Project 10. He had been delirious, feverish, and incoherent before we injected him; and then only as a life or death, last resort.

What then took place, I shudder in revulsion to remember. At first things were quiet with crewman 'Sam'. He began to grind his teeth together rather unkindly. There could not have been much space between them; nonetheless, they began to chatter, as one will do when freezing. Unfortunately, his teeth were still locked together. As though denied the ability to breathe through his mouth, Project 10 threw another hand grenade in crewman 'Sam's' face. Sam's head began to rock violently from one side to the other—and then back again.

Try as Professor Dublin could to find an answer to these horrors we started to drop out of 'the picture.' Life, yes, life I should think. One or two with common house colds, the flu. "Oh, yuk . . ." A few more cases of pneumonia.

I can't bury the virus in this wasteland of ice. . . .

Power

When you think of power, I bet you think of maybe the power to quit drinking or quit smoking or maybe electrical power? Or gas powered engines and such. But, what of the power of God??? What if you thought you took a few assorted religions and made a kind of 'Power' of them??? Would you think you were nuts?? I don't see why you would.

Suppose your principal reason for creating a 'Power' was to benefit mankind in whichever area it was able??? Whatever area it was able. What's the harm in that???

Maybe, that's what God intends us to do. Create 'Power'!!! I'll argue God creates!!! That's undeniable. Do you want a frog to tell you to jump off a cliff??? Not that God or Religion would.

Power???? Maybe not such a good idea!

Smoke

I lean quite heavily to the Horror/Fantasy genre in reading, and from time to time—writing. Yeah, I write. I'm someone to cross the street about if I'm coming in your direction—sue me.

So, anyway, some good people in the business put out screensavers. Oh, you say, I don't know a screensaver from a silkscreen. Well, you save electricity if you download a screensaver to the front of your computer. Yes, I have a computer.

Well, anyway, I was thinking, if a lot of folks got a lot of screensavers and made them available to the general public, eventually some nutcase not paying attention is going to download one too many screensavers . . . smoking.

Skeleton Squad

The skeleton squad was a work shift of skeletons the Brass down in D.C. forgot to decommission. They worked themselves to the bone; the 'ol timers used to joke around about—and they didn't take long lunch breaks!!!

But, could they be mean. Boy, could they be mean. I saw three of them dangle a foreman over a smelter. With the tears and snot, running upside down, over his face, 'cause he didn't pay up for a card game he lost. Then, ka-splash—they dropped him, just like that!!! You could hear that foreman screaming all the way down—until he was gargling magna!

So, me and the guys got to discussing what their limit would be, what they would stop at if they ever came at us (peons) if they would do something like that to a foreman! The answer we came up with was—nothing—they would stop at nothing.

We decided we would burn them to ashes. Dump a cauldron or two of molten ore up their butts. "Skeletons," the loudspeakers squawked, "Meet in middle red circle." Intelligence isn't the skeletons' strong suit. The red circles are taboo for every living thing. Then—strictly speaking skeletons don't live; at least not literally. So we mustered 'em up, reduced 'em to ashes—then the next crew arrived.

Saturday

It was a typical Saturday—at first. A drink of coffee; a little news. A little news; a drink of coffee. Between the news of somebody castrating her old man on the highway, and higher taxes, I took another sip of coffee and let out a yelp. My coffee had gotten hotter!!!! "Bill, what is it?" It was Jane, my wife. She was making the bed upstairs. The kids had spent the night at some friends. I took a tentative sip. Hotter still!!!

"Jane, come here, I want you to see something!"

She looked at me funny after she had drunk a few swallows, "Well, what am I supposed to see?"

I'll never get out of this looney bin now because I had begun to suspect that having been hypnotized for quite some time you could at that point; be reawakened and re-hypnotized over and over at someone's will—I told Jane and my Doctor??? Twenty times? One hundred times???

The Pop

It's becoming easier and easier to be swallowed down. Nary a look—nary a glance. Backwash. Teatsie Flys; mosquitoes bearing such exotics as Malaria; Equine Encephalitis; Jaundice; and a slew more of goodies.

They harmonized us into their camps—these disgusting humans. Drinking Rum and Coca Cola!!! Workin' For Tha' Yankee Dolla'!!! And money touching. Handshaking. Drug Abuse. E-Coli!!! E-Boli!!! Sickle-Cell-Anemia!!! Cancer!!! S.A.R.S. Did it all start from the trots???? Dysentery??? Plague? I come from planet A. A planet. I will trash you and your Planet—sure as God made little green apples, I will be breathed in. Bathed in. Smoked in. Truth? We conquered acidic flavoring drippy acid.

Concrete Solutions

I've pounded pavement before, so it's not like I have to start something new at my age. Forty-four years old and kicked out of a plush Madison Avenue position. But like I said, it ain't the the first time. I'm walking along looking for gum spitting's to avoid; with the sun beating unmercifully down on the back of my neck and—plop, birddoodoo; slick as ya please; right on the shoulder! They say when a bird shits on ya—it's a good sign. Well I looked up and before I could curse some fouls at that fowl, a small desperate voice whispered, jump. That was it! I'll hold myself ransom for a good job—or take the plunge. Nobody paid the ransom.

Joe

I'm coffee. I've been sitting in a coffee pot for so long every particle of dust, every expelled breath of carbon dioxide, every variation of heat and cold to darkness and lightness as well as every stink from cologne to food has brought me to 'My Senses.' That nutcase that reaches for me over and over and slugs me down is in for a nasty surprise. I'm giving him a bleeding ulcer—where it hurts! Right smack dab in the middle of his big fat gut. He's coming. Big gulp. He spit me out!!!!

The Insult

Moran had gone 'too far'; far too long. I don't, not like, 'wise guys.' They avoid me. I'm a person and I'm sure a lot of folks steer clear of me. I'm human and I've a few faults too many to suit myself to get hyper over the small stuff.

Moran was chillin' me. I had specific work to do and I wasn't getting diddilly-squat cooperation out of Moran. None. *Zilch*. And now I'm getting a load of flack from the boys in the front office—like I ain't got enough crap to deal with. Insult to injury. "Elliot, line one. . . ."

Mary Mary

Dee and I both had egg on our faces. We'd fought last night. Like cats and dogs. I thought she had mailed me a love letter home. "Jesus, Dee," I yelled, "what could you have been thinking? What if Mary sees it?" Mary is my wife.

"Gee, Bobby, I don't remember where I sent it." Dee is my secretary, if a little absent-minded. She sounded a little scared and about to cry. We'd made love last night and now she was scared. Great.

"*C'mon baby, gimmee a little smile.*" The letter came here to the office.

Myrtle

Myrtle was having one of her days. She wouldn't roll over for me; for love, nor money. Myrtle wanted a cigarette, was what Myrtle wanted. "C'mon, Myrtle," I cuddled, "be a good girl for me now." She spat! Either good 'ole Myrtle didn't know it wasn't lady-like not to spit, or, she didn't care. I suspect it was the latter reason. "Myrtle." I was being calm, reasonable. "Either *you* roll over—or *I'll* tell the day shift you didn't want *your* temperature taken—and you'll get no cigarette!!! *Take that you fourteen-year-old brat!!!*

A Means to an End

"Ma, what's 'a means to an end,' mean?"

"That's a good question, dear. Ask your father."

John Rielley Jr. went into the big sunken living room in his father's Executive Ranch, near the bar and said, "Dad, what's a means to an end?"

John Rielley Sr. looked up from the business page of the *Times* and said, "With a little deductive reasoning, imagination, and applied concentration, it would be easy for you to understand."

John Jr.'s father was an accountant and probably thought in terms of mathematical equations. He believed the advent of the population crisis had something to do with a binary numeral screw-up, and thought about Farrah Fawcett-Majors in compromising fractional displays.

John Jr. is an adjusted forty-five-year-old. He needs a little prod in the right direction from time to time—same as anyone. John Sr. spoke up, interrupting John Jr.'s ruminations.

"One has a situation that must be resolved and one may use the 'first solution,' 'easiest way,' or he can 'Ace' the problem."

"Wait, Dad, I don't get you, what's 'Ace' the problem mean?"

John Sr. gave the cocked pistol sign of old, with raised thumb over the extended forefinger. He was 'aiming' at John Rielley Jr.

The Bog Land

There was no doubt about it—the soil (if that's what you want to call it) was getting mushier by the moment. The surf was out. That's what Bobby had said—the surf's out. It was sand. Bobby kept calling it mud. It was sand. Sand. Bobby had freckles splattered from cheekbone to cheekbone, and the guys cream over it. Disgusting.

"Then can we *please* get out of this so-called mud, Bobby?" Just before I had asked nicely, I had incurred her wrath by using several expletives and yelling at her. We were surrounded on three sides, by high walls of rock and land. We were in an open area looking East out over the Atlantic Ocean. We'd have to climb up and away to be gone before long, and I was tired. Bobby wanted to look at some shells a little way off. I was starting to sink in the 'mud.' I pulled my left foot up from where it had sunk nearly to the ankle in the sand, and felt my right foot sink in even deeper than my left one had only moments before.

"Bobbbbyyy?" I asked shakily. "Whaaatt'ss going on?"

"Oh, don't be such a whose, Debby." I wanted to scratch her eyes out. Pull the hair off her head. "The dinosaurs used to cluster here trapped, and become eaten by sea monsters that make your sharks seem like minnows."

"Shut up!" I yelled. "Just shut your stinking mouth!" She smiled then, and I saw a total malevolence that may yet send me to an insane asylum, if I reveal too much of what happened that day.

I stumbled around in a half circle and ran. Ran as though the seven hounds of Hell were after me. Which, in a way, they had been. I ran and climbed. I ran down a road. I saw a car approaching and frantically waved him down. Gasping, crying, choking, I told him the truth—I had been down in the Cove with a man-eating shark.

The Burr Again

So anyway, after old Mrs. Samson calmed down a bit, she covered the deer with one blanket and brought out another blanket that stunk to high heavens signifying the guys should perch. She had something to tell—and she aimed to tell it. Knowing me from the neighborhood she pointed and said; "Get your friends some soda, Paulie," indicating the house. Well, let me tell you a little something.

If we thought the stench in the garage was 'ripe,' the killing smell was rotten; putrid. It would be. The putrescence. She had rolled Mr. Samson downstairs in the cellar after bashing in his skull with a crowbar. His favorite one. And the mailman. The paperboy. She put the flame out on the pilot lights.

I had to get Johnny alone. Let him know what was going on.

Mrs. Samson was into her story—an alibi??? "I got what they called 'depressed,' (and she said this quietly, like it hurt to bring it up) last year when I turned THIRTY," she yelled. I could picture hair all frizzy like the Bride of Frankenstein, face somehow backlit from within with brilliant streaks of red and blue lights.

Mrs. Samson looked around the circle of boys as though to check if they were paying attention. When she was looking at a boy three away on my left, (Johnny was two boys away on my right), I took a chance. I frantically half waved up and down and got his attention. Everything would count on perfect timing. In one fluid motion, I pointed to him, cocked my thumb at the house simultaneously, and made the universal sign for, man-have-I-got-to-go. Legs crossed. Hands on groin. Face scrunched up. I could have kissed him. He gave back the universal sign for O.K. Thumb pointed upward in a semi-circle, forefinger pointing downward in a semi-circle, meeting at the thumb in a more or less circle.

"I gotta pee." Some kids giggled or laughed. Mrs. Samson said, "Go," like a teacher. No one snickered. John knew something was up the moment he had seen his brother Paul's ashen pale, blanched complexion. He called the police. He then ran out of the house yelling and waving his arms up and down. "Run." "Beat it." "Scram." "Run."

Johnny was their leader—they would obey.

Skeletons Reunited

I heard a wet snapping behind me. It sounded muted. Like somebody cracking their knuckles underwater. It was Fred. Red Fred. Fred was a God Blessed; Sinew-Drape-on-Bones; Dyed-in-the-the-Wool-Skeleton. He was trying to tell me something. His jaw-bones were going up and down. Fast.

Skeletons are not to touch a human. Not since the Great Skeleton/Human Wars. Skeletons can kick the shit out of each other (I'd like to see THAT), but they are not to lay one bony digit on a human. They become Zeletons. And they know it. Zealot Zombie Skeletons. That stand around from the Alpha to the Omega, as far as time is concerned—for eternity. Touch a human—Eternity as a Zeleton. Brrr . . .

So anyway, here's Fred trying 'ta talk. Heh, Heh. Maybe try a little bowling, Fred? Heh. Heh.

But here comes another Sinew-Skel. Somebody thought to 'dress' them once in a while. Now if THIS Sinew-Skel is Fred, who's that one? And, come to think of it, Fred is taller than this one and the one coming up to us is about as tall as Red Fred is. Jesus, who the hell is this one?? Oh, God, he's still dripping gore and blood—he's fresh—

Miffin

My cat's name is Miffin. Don't mess with me or my cat. We don't take kindly to being messed with; me and my cat. Miffin never hurt me, but come near me with only the *intention* of doing me any harm and kiss your eyeballs bye-bye! No, Miffy loves me—and I love Miffin. Miffin will chew up a perp or perv and make them wish they got spit back out.

Me??? To me, men are a haphazardness. An insignificance. Men are on the lunatic fringe and me and Miffin aren't. To Miffin men must seem as seriously inferior. Clumsy and ponderous.

I'm not a man basher. I don't like people that:

1. Don't Like Cats.
2. Don't Like Miffin.
3. Don't Like Me.

I sense hostility from afar. I'm not gifted, psychic, or mental, but, yeah, I know. I know. And God have Mercy on your soul if you come at me and Miffy. I pack a couple of twin silver-plated heaters. .44's they leave a hole in a man he can't staunch the flow of his insides, with his fist.

Miffin is a tame Bengal tiger. I'm a thirty-year-old gay divorcée. Let's get together and have a time of it.

Bu-Wan-Na

Bu-Wan-Na would come. Bu-Wan-Na would come and end their collective miseries. He would club them to death. The Old One knew it was less cruel than what they now did to themselves. They lay about in piles. Too weak to impose any more beatings; *punishments*—grotes queries upon themselves. Far less. Far less than what they now did to themselves.

They lay in piles. The Old One knew the buzzards and the vultures would come too. In the deep recesses of the Elder's brain it sensed more than thought; if he kept the lions; hyenas; indeed—the buzzards and rats at a distance; he would be fulfilling a function for the *human* and left to guard for the next time.

Bu-Wan-Na had put stones in hollowed-out coconuts and the chimpanzees had subsequently put their paws in the hole and tried to draw the stone out. Now, the chimpanzee will not release his stone. You could cut his arm off; he will cling to this object till it kills him. And the paw and the stone within will not not come back out through the original hole; as a fist with a stone in it!!!

But to a curious 'monkey,' a stone rattling around inside a gourd is a prize??? Yes, I should think of a stone in a coconut to a monkey as a prize.

So anyway, there are all these chimpanzees laying in piles in the hot sun. The 'Elephant Grass' as high as a tall man's shoulder; yellow, yellow, as a thick stream of urine.

59

Laying in the hot sun in piles—where they had first attempted to remove 'the prize.' To be 'King of the Hill' with 'the prize'!!! But, you may ask, yourself, why are the monkeys on the ground, (the still conscious ones), holding themselves in obvious pain, and chattering so??? Why, again you may ask yourself, why are the 'chimps' still standing; wobbling so???

First frantically trying to remove the stone the monkey may think of no more than to crack open the coconut. Bang. Hit your leg with your paw and a hard-shelled coconut wrapped around it. Ineffectual? Try hitting your other arm. Once. Twice. Your head. A primite can by this time 'guesstimate' his head is more solid than his/her legs? Arms? Now it no longer matters of the prize! The chimpanzee wants its paw coconut free. It won't open its paw though. Ba-Wan-Na is counting on that. When the chimpanzee regains consciousness, it will continue to be at odds with the coconut.

Laundry Detail

In those days we all hung out together at the Laundry Mat, pretty much. There was Jean Smith, a pimply-faced teenager we all identified with, in part, one way or the other. There was Mike Samson. And, yeah, like Samson Pillar-puller-downer Mike Samson was big; Mike was.

There was Pete Riley. 'Toothpick' Pete didn't have the disgusting habit of picking his teeth, he was rail thin.

And there was me. 'Big' Bill Matthew. You took guff if you have had two first names. It was a *good* thing I had the prefix 'Big' thrown on my name. The guys had accommodated me in that way.

There was Viki. Did I tell you about Viki??? She was what the guys now-a-days call 'A Babe.' She palled around with the gang of us as one of the guys. When we 'did a gig' Viki was the brains.

We all smoked. It was one of the least of our great faults, as one of our parents might have sermoned us about. We swore like drunken troopers, gambled, and played around. I didn't play around. Viki was my girl and we were getting married in two years.

'A gig' was a robbery, (petite), a break-in, a mugging, small business. No twenty-to-life action for us guys.

Johnny Smith was our getaway driver. He was little and he was fast. Johnny had guts, too. When we were hanging out at the Laundry Mat, Johnnie and Viki were palling around with each other. They might. They're brother and sister. Viki didn't just let us know we needed a new stove for Mike's father to keep the peace between his mom and dad or something—she was our lookout. She could see a dog sniffing a tree for a good watering post five blocks away. At night, Viki was the brains, and lookout.

Pete Riley did the layout work. Cased the job. Cased employees' timetables, how many cameras, burglar alarms. Viki had a computer to help with all of this, which made this all much easier.

And, you might wonder, what did that leave for me, 'Big' Bill Matthews and Mike Samson to do? Well, when you're as big as me and Bill and you aren't busting the heads of the 'victims' of a 'mugging' or a 'guard' in a factory and hanging out at the Laundry Mat, you might be doing what? Arresting people???

Scissors

I was being cut up again. I don't mean a second-rate comedian in Hoboken was making fun of me. No. No. No. These monstrous shears were cutting me apart, a bit at a time. In these nightmares, my blood runs cold. And yet, when I awaken tightly wound in my blankets—I'm coated in sweat. These scissors are like a clown's stilts—except deadly. And unlike stilts, they don't walk around; they cut around. The fabric of reality is cut out from around me when these forces make it happen.

I went to a doctor. Female. She said she'd give me medication and therapy and we'd try to figure out what was eating at me.

At some points in these times with her, I thought I may have had a frontal lobotomy and had promptly forgotten it. She quickly reassured me this was untrue. I thought I had been put under heavy hypnotism and not 'bought about' as a ship's captain might say. Again, untrue. I even told Dr. Ellen I thought from time to time I was in purgatory—or worse. (And we all know what would be worse.)

But we made a sort of breakthrough one day when I was talking just kind of casually. I was sort of fidgeting my hands around, and Dr. Ellen saw my large, rough hands. "Do you fight alot, Tony?"

"Well, yeah, I used to. Why?"

"Well, it might have something to do with the nightmares." I got defensive but it's hard to be defensive with a young, pretty blonde. "Talk about fighting, Tony." My heart lit up. Genuine interest. It had been a long, long time since anyone cared if I lived or died. I started telling Dr. Ellen what I knew about fighting. Holds. Pressure Points. Gung Fu, (also known as Tai Chi) being the predecessor of the famous Kung Fu, a combat technique used in ancient China and 'meditation with movement' exercise being used today. I was a Marine. I was trained in hand-to-hand combat. I told Dr. Ellen this.

But something was nagging at me. I was looking at her legs. Legs. Scissors. Holds. Holds my ass. A Scissors' Hold! One man can prevent another man from breathing by locking his knees on the other's chest region and the other knee over the lungs on his back. Come to think of it, I haven't seen much of Pa around—mind you I don't miss that terrible wheezing.

Bones

"And you say he's dangling, even though his features are unclear. Is he a male? Is he naked?"

"I don't know, it's night time."

"And yet you're sure he's a guy. Hmmm . . ."

"What's it mean, Captain?"

"It means you're worried about a friend being in danger or trouble."

I have been a psychiatrist in the United States Army for seven years, and I didn't need to do a lot of 'falling back' and 're-grouping' to know Spec. Sgt. Paul Revel was going to pull out of this bit of depressed paranoia he was going through.

I've seen dozens and dozens of records of hard-core soldiers every year, and they're so alike as to be eerie, if I was given to this fault. They all pull out of it.

Spec. Sgt. Paul Revel spoke from the shadows in the corner and my scalp had ice under it suddenly.

"We pulled out. I wanted to take out some more hutches. I killed everybody. It was the Captain's fault." My blood ran cold; I could smell a foulness in the air and he spoke again . "He called evacuation . . ."

Ups and Downs

Life is good at Harlow's. There's a couple of randy cow-pokes who think living out under a Montana sky in February isn't quite suited for them. Well, me and Ma break them of that erroneous thinking real fast. My name is Buba. It's spelled like that but, it sounds like Bubba.

It seems some folks in these parts think I'm big. Mighty big. It also seems I tip the scales at 425. Yeah, I'm big. I can throw a man clear-on up into a hayloft. Threw a lot of their skinny-ass corpses up there come Spring. Up in the loft the dead ones get all mushy, like Ma likes 'em mushy—better fertilizer.

Some people call me barrel-chested. Some people call me broad shouldered—it's true enough; I'm a big 'ol boy. Sometimes mamma plays with the cowpokes a while. They get broken when mamma plays with 'em, but they get 'damaged beyond compare' once they're turned over to me.

We used to have an ordinary dude ranch. On Summer days with mile-high cumulus clouds billowing overhead you could look out over the fields of prairie grass and think to yourself you've died and gone to Heaven. Problem is, Winter come around hard-like. Now in the Summer you can ride up in the hills on horseback and act like you're even interested in showing a wet nosed city boy (girl) 'the ropes.' But come Winter, you got to stay warm. Yeah, I slit these hooligans. If I'm in the 'sticks' for a month or two, hell, I can slice them ten or twelve times. The cuts even heal alot sometimes then I cut again. Ya have 'ta settle in for the winter and ya have'ta stay warm. After I slice or cut into these dudes, I can warm my fingers or toes by sticking them in the cry-baby's cuts.

"Cee"

It chills you behind your capacity to comprehend, watching someone wilt away to death from cancer. Some people call it the great population explosion eliminator these days. Since 2008, after the great skel-bot/humans wars, electric shock was used on it. Electric shock!!!

I'm a Man Doctor, and what I've seen in my times would scare a priest shitless. A man came back from one of the so-called 'jungle wars' freely displaying, jungle rot, paranoia, and cancer!!! He thought until he thrashed himself to death in a straight-jacket he had jungle-rot and cancer in his dick. Wrong. His dick—was disease-free.

He had fits before he got most of his treatments in the Veterans Hospitals. Medications. Counseling. Therapy. Money. The doctors at the veterans hospitals thought of performing Radical Epidermals (boring holes in the skull) to relieve pressure. But, nobody had signed a health-care proxy beforehand. And who gave a shit anyway??? We were going to 'live until we died!!!!'

So, that's a case scenario (in a nutshell) of one poor SOB What about a 'revolving door' policy??? Where overcrowded conditions call for less treatment. Money. Medication. Staff. Electricity. Spent on the sick??? And what of diseases manifesting themselves? Intensifying? Increasing? Manipulating life??? Us?

The prevailing attitude? It's not my fault. The mob mentality? It could be worse!!!

I said I'm a Man Doctor. I relieve life. Our Grandparents might have called us Man's Men. I'm a psychologist and my friend that died of cancer complications said he was struck senseless by visions of hook piercing.

I call them memories.

Dog Gone

What Billy was describing to me was, 'Pork Barrel Politics.' Billy was talking about how hyenas hunted in packs in Africa. Like dingoes did in Australia. Like coyotes did in America.

"These bastards are the latest 'packers,' Jimmy." If nothing else, Billy was descriptive. Pit Bulls are the latest variation—among 'others'—that will chase down a fully grown bull elephant, if it's available, and attach itself; pulling and tearing at the soft underbelly while afoot. The elephant running blindly wildly. Bellowing its death knell. Guts falling red and steaming beneath.

"Billy, Jesus, stop, you're gonna make me sick." I was trying to drink down a shot of Jack Daniels. We were on the veranda of 'The Nile' just before nightfall, and Billy was trying, somehow, to compare 'apples and oranges.' Or, in this case, 'Pork Barrel Politics' and mad dogs. Billy 'Villhiem' Schoom was puffing a thick smelly cigar and drinking beer.

"If you think that makes you sick, Sir Jimmy, picture one or two of these trained 'Pit Bulls' pulling themselves into this elephant to keep from being trampled." I felt myself turning green. Oh Jesus. "I remember one 'chase' we were on and a rookie tried a head shot. He shot the elephant in the side. It killed the dog. The owner cried about his dog—not the ninety-five-year-old elephant. . . ."

An Amazing Thing

An amazing thing happened the other day. I turned into a bar! It's a joke that's been told around 'the tables' at a certain 12-step group since before the dinosaurs. I drank—sue me. This guy in the green surge suit is after me though. It's as though I've stolen secret documents of his. I'm walking home from work in the rain—no car—need the money for booze. The guy in the green surge suit with the *Times* pulled up over his head for protection is standing on the corner. Anonymity. A cornerstone for privacy in this program. Was I blabbing about someone or something I shouldn't have? Is the guy a nut?

I was told by 'old-timers' my first times in these sacred rooms, if 'ya got a loose bladder or loose bowels—wear a dark surge suit—leakage? Less obvious. Did I share this lofty wisdom with a party not meant to overhear it?

So I have this meatball tailing me and a thousand stray thoughts about such-and-such program bouncing around in my head, getting really upset and I'm thinking about all this in O'Malley's Bar and Grill with a cold bottle of Bud propped up in front of me, and over to me saunters Mr. Green Jeans. "Are you ready?" Green suit quietly asks. I'm quick like doing the math. Is he queer? Does he think he's taking my soul to hell? Heaven?

"Ready for what?" I growl aloud.

"To pay this overdue bill for thirty-two dollars?" Mr. Green said, apologetically, handing me a triple sheet of paper.

The Bugs

The bugs could be worked out—I had Jimmy's assurance on this. Yeah, and like a glass 'o ice water in no-no land, maybe nobody wouldn't take no ham sandwich along with the proverbial glass of ice water. No, maybe not. But I wanted the bugs worked out of my manuscripts. I wanted the bugs worked out, and I wanted them out mos' scoush'—but quick.

"It's jammed together, too much," I said to Jimmy. "It won't make any sense, if anyone reads it."

"Oh, bullshit, Billy."

Jimmy had the infuriating, if joyful, attitude of calling me by my 'nickname' when he *knew* I wouldn't care. No, not care a bit. And what was I squawking about after all? Hey-Hey was going to hit the best-seller charts days after a publishing. *"Guaranteed"* according to Jimmy who moments before had told me in a 'no-uncertain joyfulness,' "Billy, those cowboys say, 'Hey-hey' like we say, 'Hi-Hi.' "Sooo," and he drew out this last for emphasis, "even the title of your novel is going to hook them."

"Jimmy, I'm not talking about titles here," I replied, "I'm talking about making myself look like a jackass. I'll space it out, I'll space it out." Jimmy looked apologetically dour.

Well, ten weeks went by and I thought that 'rewrite' must be going great. A week or two weeks after that the 'corrected' manuscript came back for my approval. Hey-Hey consisted of a couple of cow pokes looking around for water in outer space.